G000278777

Published 1984 by WOLFHOUND PRESS
68 Mountjoy Square, Dublin 1.

These stories have previously appeared
in separate editions in 1977.

British Library Cataloguing in Publication Data
O'Flaherty, Liam
The test of courage; and, All things come of age.
I. Title II. O'Flaherty, Liam. All things come of age.
823'.912[J] PZ7

ISBN 0-86327-044-1 Pbk

This book is published with the financial assistance of
The Arts Council / An Chomhairle Ealaíon, Ireland.
Printed in Ireland by O'Brien Promotions Ltd., Dublin.

Masterpieces for Children

LIAM O'FLAHERTY

All Things Come of Age
and
The Test of Courage

Illustrated by Terence O'Connell

Wolfhound Press

The baby rabbit was sitting in the sun just by the entrance to his burrow. He was half asleep. His big ears sloped along his back and his sides heaved gently with his breathing. Now and again a slight breeze came up from the stream, raised the brown fur on his side and made silver furrows in it. When the breeze touched him, he sniffed the air and wanted his mother to come and feed him.

He was now big enough to graze for his own food along the fertile bank of the stream, but all his brothers and sisters had been killed by a weasel and for that reason there was still enough milk in his mother's drying udder to feed him. So he had not yet been forced to pluck the short blades of grass with his teeth and chew them. All he did was to come out of his burrow, hop about in the sun, smelling the ground, or sit attentively listening to sound, until something menacing came to his ears and he dived into his burrow for shelter.

At the moment, there was perfect peace by the bank of the stream. The sun was still at its height, although it was long past noon. It shone full on the waterfall, that poured with a wild, sad murmur from a narrow gorge, lined with a thick growth of flowering heather. Like a widespread horse's mane, the water poured from the gorge, thick and brown at its base, where it was coloured by the earth and heather and then, falling, it widened out into a silver sheet. There was a long, deep pool below the fall. Flies skimmed its surface and trout leaped at their gaudy wings. At the near end of the pool, just beneath where the little rabbit dozed, there was a line of boulders thrown across the stream. A wild duck stood on one leg in a hollow between two of the boulders. The duck was asleep, with its bill tucked under one wing.

All was still, except for the drowsy music of the waterfall. Some time ago, when the duck swooped down, quacking, onto the boulders, the little rabbit had taken fright and darted into his burrow. But when he peered out again and watched the duck for a long time, as it fed in the stream, prodding with its beak, he became used to the bird and feared it no more. Now it was asleep and it had become part of the surroundings. There was nothing to be seen of it between the boulders, except its flashing wing feathers and a little of its yellow beak.

Suddenly the duck awoke and withdrew its bill from beneath its wing. It raised its neck and turned its head from side to side, listening. Then it began to bob its head and put both feet on the ground. It moved a little to one side, jerking its head and its tail. Then it quacked. It was a low quack, scarcely audible, but it startled the little rabbit. He became wide awake and moved. At first he laid his ears flat along his back and bent down low to the earth on his stomach. Then he raised himself gradually, thrust forward his ears and listened. He watched the duck.

Now the duck was very excited and began to quack continuously. Shaking its gullet, it paddled about on the boulder, taking tiny steps. The little rabbit became very curious, because he failed to discover the cause of the bird's unrest. There was neither sound nor smell. He raised himself on his haunches, thrust his ears as far forward as he could and let his forelegs drop along his breast. He listened and watched intently. He began to get afraid.

Then the duck uttered a loud quack and swept from the boulders with a great swishing of its wings. It swung in a half circle and then shot upwards into the sky, gathering speed as it rose, until it disappeared over a clump of trees farther down the bank of the stream. The rabbit dropped his forelegs to the ground and gathered himself together to make a dive into his burrow. Yet he did not move. The swoop of the duck and the loud swishing of its wings had so startled him that he could not move. So he remained where he was, crouching.

And then, as he lay crouching, he began to feel afraid. It was the same feeling he experienced a few days previously, when his last remaining brother, having hopped into the clump of briars on the left, had suddenly begun to scream. There was a strange feeling in the air, the nearness of a sinister force, that prevented movement. At that time, however, he had been able to move after a little while and run into his burrow. Now it was different.

The sinister feeling increased. There was absolute silence and there was nothing strange to smell and yet he felt the approach of the sinister force, something unknown and monstrous. In spite of himself, although he wanted awfully to hide from it, he looked in the direction whence he sensed the approach of the enemy. His head shook violently as he glanced towards the boulders that lay across the stream. And then he began to scream. A weasel was crossing the line of boulders.

The baby rabbit had never before seen a weasel, but the long brown body, that moved with awful speed, making no sound, drove him crazy with horror. The weasel paused in the middle of the stream, raised his powerful head and stared at the rabbit, his wicked eyes fixed. And then, keeping his head raised and his eyes on his prey, he glided like a flash to the bank. He disappeared for a fraction of a second behind a stone in his path and then appeared again, standing against the little stone, staring fixedly. Now his powerful head, raised above the long brown barrel of his body, was like the boss of a hammer, poised to strike. The rabbit's screaming became wilder. He was now completely in the brute's power, mesmerized by the staring eyes and by the sinister presence.

The weasel, having mesmerized his prey, was on the point of gliding forward to his meal of blood, when the baby rabbit's mother dashed from the clump of briars on the left, screaming as she ran. She moved in a strange fashion, leaping sideways like a dog trying to sight a hare in a field of corn. It was a grotesque dance, to the accompaniment of wild screams. She passed directly in front of the weasel and circled him twice, threatening him each time with her upraised paws. She drew his eyes from her little one towards herself. When they were fixed on her, she dropped to the ground and began to tremble. She crawled away slowly towards the clump of briars, continuing the while to scream. Then she lay down. The weasel slid from the stone and moved towards her swiftly.

As soon as the weasel's eyes left him, the baby rabbit stopped screaming. Then he began to crawl away

upstream. He moved as if his back were hurt. He was almost paralysed and it hurt him terribly to draw his hind legs up under his belly in order to hop forward. But the farther away he went from the weasel, the lesser grew the pain in his joints, until at last it seemed that a weight was lifted from his body and he was able to run, staggering a little, into a great hummock of grass that grew around a gorse bush. He bored a hole through the long, coarse grass with his snout and then lay still in the very middle of it, panting. There he fell asleep.

When he awoke it was late in the evening and the sun had set. He felt very hungry. By now, his paroxysm of fear and the weasel's staring eyes were only a vague memory. He wanted to suck his mother and satisfy his hunger. He backed out of his lair in the grass to look for her. He would find her in the burrow where she always fed him in the evening.

He ran back to the burrow as fast as he could, the little white button of his tail hopping as he ran in the twilight like a ball of cotton carried on the wind. He dived eagerly into the burrow and searched for her. The burrow was empty. He came out again, sat on his haunches and raised his ears, smelling and listening. In the distance, frogs were croaking in a marsh. A curlew called on the wing. A

multitude of other birds, about to perch for the night, were warbling. He dropped his forelegs and hopped about, smelling the ground, now and again thrusting forward one ear and then another, listening. All round the mouth of the burrow, among the thrown out earth, that was pebbled with round droppings, he could smell her, but the smell was old and faint. He went farther from the hole, nosing the ground, in search of a fresher scent.

At last he found one, the track on which she had danced before the weasel. He followed it carefully, round and round, until he came to her, over near the clump of briars. She was lying on her side, already stiff in death. Her udder was towards him and he was on the point of thrusting at the nearest teat with his snout, when he drew back slightly, astonished at the unusual odour which her body exuded. He crouched, with his head close into his neck. Then he thrust forward his head once more timidly, and gently smelt her, all along her body. Just beneath her ear the smell was very strange and terrifying. There was a little hole there and the rim of the hole was clotted with dried blood. As soon as he sniffed the blood, the paroxysm of fear returned. He leaped backwards, sat up on his hind legs, stared at the corpse, squealed and fled to his burrow. He lay in the innermost corner of it, panting.

For a long time he lay there, his head pressed hard against the cold earth. Then again, hunger began to gnaw at his bowels. His hunger gradually became stronger than his fear, driving out the memory of the horrid, clotted blood, around the hole beneath his mother's ear. He forgot his mother. His hunger grew fierce, drowning memory. He crawled out of the burrow.

Night had now fallen and the moon was out, gilding the grassy slope with a fairy light. Several rabbits from neighbouring burrows were grazing in the moonlight. Two little ones, about his own age, were chasing one another. He hopped over to them and began to nibble at the grass.

Dew was now falling on the grass, making it juicy and sweet, just like his mother's milk. When he had eaten his fill, he joined in the dance of the other little rabbits. Now he was no longer afraid and he had completely forgotten his mother. He was one of the herd.

THE TEST OF COURAGE

Liam O'Flaherty

WOLFHOUND PRESS

THE TEST OF COURAGE

At sundown on a summer evening, Michael O'Hara and Peter Cooke left their village with great secrecy. Crouching behind fences, they made a wide circuit and then ran all the way to a little rock-bound harbour that lay a mile to the southwest. They carried their caps in their hands as they ran and they panted with excitement. They were about to execute a plan of adventure which they had devised for weeks. They were going to take Jimmy the weaver's boat out for a night's bream fishing.

Michael O'Hara was twelve years and four months, five months younger than his comrade. He had very intelligent eyes of a deep-blue colour and his fair hair stood up on end like close-cropped bristles. He looked slender and rather delicate in his blue jersey and grey flannel trousers that only reached half way down his bare shins. Although it was he who had conceived and planned the adventure, just as he planned all the adventures of the two comrades, he now lagged far behind in the race to the port. This was partly due to his inferior speed. It was also due to a nervous reaction against embarking on an expedition that would cause grave anxiety to his parents.

Peter Cooke looked back after reaching the great mound of boulders that lined the head of the harbour. He frowned and halted when he saw his companion far behind. His sturdy body seemed to be too large for his clothes, which were identical with those worn by O'Hara. His hair was black and curly. His face was freckled. He had the heavy jaws and thick nose of a fighter. His small grey eyes, set close together, lacked the intelligence of Michael O'Hara's eyes.

'Hurry on,' he cried in a loud whisper, when Michael came closer, 'What ails you? Are you tired already?'

Michael looked back over his shoulder furtively.

'I thought I saw somebody,' he said in a nervous tone.

'Who?' said Peter. 'Who did you see?'

'Over there,' Michael said.

He pointed towards the north in the direction of the village, which was now half hidden by the intervening land. Only the thatched roofs and the smoking chimneys of the houses were visible. The smoke rose straight up from the chimneys in the still twilight. To the west of the village ran a lane, its low fence standing out against the fading horizon of the sky like a curtain full of irregular holes.

'I think it was my mother I saw coming home from milking the cow along the lane,' Michael said in a voice that was slightly regretful. 'I just saw her head over the fence, but it looked like her shawl. I don't think she saw me, though. Even if she did see me, she wouldn't know who it was.'

'Come on,' Peter said. 'She couldn't see you that far

away. We have to hurry or it will be dark before we get the curragh in the water.'

As nimbly as goats, the two boys ran down the sloping mound of granite boulders and along the flat stretch of grey limestone that reached out to the limit of the tide. Then they went into a cave beneath a low cliff that bordered the shore. They brought the gear they had hidden in this cave down to the sea's edge and dropped it at the point where they were to launch the boat.

'Do you think we'll be able to carry her down, Peter?' Michael said, as they ran back across the mound of boulders to fetch the boat.

Peter halted suddenly and looked at his comrade. He was irritated by the nervous tone of Michael's voice.

'Are you getting afraid?' he said roughly.

'Who? Me?' said Michael indignantly.

'If you are,' said Peter, 'say the word and we'll go back home. I don't want to go out with you if you start whinging.'

'Who's whinging?' Michael said. 'I only thought we mightn't be able to carry her down to the rock. Is there any harm in that?'

'Come on,' said Peter, 'and stop talking nonsense. Didn't we get under her four times to see could we raise her? We raised her, didn't we? If we could raise her, we can carry her. Jimmy the weaver can rise under her all by himself and he's an old man. He's such a weak old man, too, that no crew in the village would take him out fishing with them. It would be a shame if the two of us weren't as strong as Jimmy the weaver.'

'I hope he won't put a curse on us,' Michael said as they walked along, 'when he finds out that we took his curragh. He's terrible for cursing when he gets angry. I've seen him go on his two knees and curse when two eggs were stolen from under his goose and she hatching. He pulled up his trousers and cursed on his naked knees.'

'He'd be an ungrateful man,' Peter said, 'if he put a curse on us after all we've done for him during the past week. Four times we drew water from the well for him. We dug potatoes for him in his little garden twice and we gave him a rabbit that we caught. The whole village would throw stones at his house if he put a curse on us after we doing all that for him.'

All the village boats usually rested on the flat ground behind the mound of granite boulders. There was a little wall of loose stones around each boat to protect it from the great south winds that sometimes blew in from the ocean. At present only the weaver's boat remained in its stone pen, lying bottom up within its protecting wall, with stone props under the transoms to keep it from the ground. All the other pens were empty, for it was the height of the bream season and the men were at sea.

"Come on now,' Peter said when they reached the boat. 'Lift up the bow.'

They got on each side of the bow and raised it without difficulty.

“You get under it now and settle yourself,’ Peter said.

Michael crouched and got under the boat, with his face towards the stern. He rested his shoulders against the front seat and braced his elbows against the frame. Although they had practiced raising the boat, he now began to tremble lest he might not be able to bear the weight when Peter raised the stern.

‘Keep your legs well apart,’ Peter said, ‘and stand loose same as I told you.’

‘I’m ready,’ Michael said nervously. ‘You go ahead and raise her.’

Peter put on his cap with the peak turned backwards. Then he set himself squarely under the stern of the boat. He gritted his teeth and made his strong back rigid. Then he drew in a deep breath and made a sudden effort. He raised the boat and then spread his legs to distribute the weight. Both boys staggered for a few moments, as they received the full weight of the boat on their shoulders.

‘Are you balanced?’ Peter said.
‘Go ahead,’ said Michael.

Peter led the way, advancing slowly with the rhythmic movement of his body which he had copied from his elders. He held his body rigid above the hips, which swayed as he threw his legs forward limply in an outward arc. As each foot touched the ground, he lowered his hips and then raised them again with the shifting of weight to the other foot.

Michael tried to imitate this movement, but he was unable to do it well owing to his nervousness. In practice he had been just as good as Peter. Now, however, the memory of his mother's shawled head kept coming into his mind to disturb him.

'Try to keep in step,' Peter called out, 'and don't grip the frame. Let your shoulders go dead.'

'I'm doing my best,' Michael said, 'but it keeps shifting on my shoulders.'

'That's because you're taking a grip with your hands. Let your shoulders go dead.'

They were both exhausted when they finally laid down the boat on the weed-covered rock by the sea's edge. They had to rest a little while. Then they gently pushed the boat into the water over the smooth carpet of red weed. They had to do this very carefully, because the coracle was just a light frame of thin pine lathes covered with tarred canvas. The least contact with a sliver of stone, or even with a limpet cone, would have put a hole in the canvas. Fortunately the sea was dead calm, and they managed the launching without accident.

'Now, in God's name,' Peter said, imitating a man's voice as he dipped his hand in the seawater and made the Sign of the Cross on his forehead according to ritual, 'I'll go aboard and put her under way. You hand in the gear when I bring her stern to shore.'

He got into the prow seat, unshipped the oars and dipped the glambs in the water before fixing them on the thole pins. Then he manoeuvred the stern of the boat face to the rock. Michael threw aboard the gear, which included a can of half-baited limpets for bait, four lines coiled on small wooden frames, half a loaf of bread rolled up in a piece of cloth, and the anchor rope with a large granite stone attached. Then he also dipped his right hand in the brine water and made the Sign of the Cross on his forehead.

'In God's name,' he said reverently, as he put one knee on the stern and pushed against the rock with this foot, 'head her out.'

As Peter began to row, Michael took his seat on the after transom and unshipped his oars. He dipped the glambs in the water and put the oars on the thole pins.

'Face land, right hand underneath,' Peter called out just like a grownup captain giving orders to his crew.

'I'm with you,' Michael said. 'Head her out.'

The two boys rowed well, keeping time perfectly. Soon they had cleared the mouth of the little harbour and they were in the open sea. Night was falling, but they could see the dark cluster of village boats beneath a high cliff to the west. They turned east.

'Take a mark now and keep her straight,' Peter said.

Michael brought two points on the dim land to the west into line with the stern and they rowed eastwards until they came abreast of a great pile of rock that had fallen from the cliff. Here they cast anchor. When they had tied

the anchor rope to the cross-stick in the bow, the boat swung round and became motionless on the still water.

'Oh! You devil!' Peter said excitedly. 'Out with the lines now and let us fish. Wouldn't it be wonderful if we caught a boat load of bream. We'd be the talk of the whole parish.'

'Maybe we will,' cried Michael, equally excited.

Now he was undisturbed by the memory of his mother's shawled head. Nor was he nervous about his position, out at night on a treacherous ocean in a frail coracle. The wild rapture of adventure had taken full possession of him.

Such was the haste with which they baited and paid out their lines that they almost transfixed their hands with the hooks. Each boy paid out two lines, one on either side of the boat. They had cast anchor right in the midst of a school of bream. Peter was the first to get his lines into water. They had barely sunk when he got a strike on both of them.

'Oh! You devil!' he cried. 'I've got two.'

In his excitement he tried to haul the two lines simultaneously and lost both of the soft-lipped fish. In the meantime, Michael also got a strike on one of his lines. He swallowed his breath and hauled rapidly. A second fish struck while he was hauling the first line. He also became greedy and grabbed the second line, letting the first fish escape. But he landed the second fish.

'Oh! Peter,' he cried, 'we'll fill the boat like you said.'

He put the fish smartly between his knees and pulled the hook from its mouth. He dropped it on the bottom of the boat, where it began to beat a tattoo with its tail.

'Oh! You devil!' Peter cried. 'The sea is full of them.'

He had again thrown his lines into the water and two fish immediately impaled themselves on the hooks. This time he landed both fish, as the lessening of excitement enabled him to use his skill.

'We should have brought more limpets,' Michael said, 'This lot we brought won't be half enough!'

The fish continued to strike. Despite losing a large percentage, they had caught thirty-five before an accident drove the boat away from the school. A light breeze had come up from the land. It hardly made a ripple on the surface of the sea, yet its impact caused the boat to lean away from the restraint of the anchor rope. The rope went taut. Then the anchor stone slipped from the edge of a reef on which it had dropped. Falling into deeper water, it could not find ground. The boat swung round and began to drift straight out to sea, pressed by the gentle breeze.

The two boys, intent on their fishing, did not notice the accident. Soon, however, the fish ceased to strike. They did not follow the boat into deep water. The lines hung idly over the sides.

'They're gone,' Michael said. 'Do you think it's time for us to go home?'

We can't go home yet,' Peter said indignantly. 'We have

only thirty-five fish yet. Wait until they begin to strike again when the tide turns. Then you'll see that we'll fill the boat. In any case, we can't go back until the moon rises. It's too dark now to make our way past the reef.'

'It's dark all right,' Michael said in a low voice. 'I can't see land, although it's so near.'

Now that the fish had gone away, the vision of his mother's shawled head returned to prick his conscience, and the darkness frightened him as it always did. Yet he dared not insist on trying to make port, lest Peter might think he was a coward.

'They'll start biting again,' Peter continued eagerly. 'You wait and see. We'll fill the boat. Then the moon will be up and it will be lovely rowing into port. Won't they be surprised when they see all the fish we have? They won't say a word to us when we bring home that awful lot of fish.'

Michael shuddered on being reminded of the meeting with his parents after this escapade.

'I'm hungry,' he said. 'Do you think we should eat our bread? No use bringing it back home again.'

'I'm hungry, too,' Peter said. 'Let's eat the bread while we're waiting for the tide to turn.'

They divided the half loaf and began to eat ravenously. When they had finished, Michael felt cold and sleepy.

'We should have brought more clothes to put on us,' he said. 'The sea gets awful cold at night, doesn't it?'

'Let's lie up in the bow,' Peter said, 'I feel cold myself. We'll lie together in the shelter of the bow while we're waiting for the tide to turn. That way we won't feel the cold in the shelter of the bow.'

They lay down in the bow side by side. There was just room enough for their two bodies stretched close together.

'It's much warmer this way sure enough,' Michael said sleepily.

'It's just like being in bed,' Peter said. 'Oh! You devil! When I grow up I'll be a sailor. Then I can sleep every night out in the middle of the sea.'

They fell asleep almost at once. In their sleep they put their arms about one another. The moon rose and its eerie light fell on them, as they lay asleep in the narrow bow, rocked gently by the boat's movement, to the soft music of the lapping water. The moonlight fell on the dark sides of the boat that drifted before the breeze. It shone on the drifting lines that hung from the black sides, like the tentacles of an evil monster that was carrying the sleeping boys out far over the empty ocean. The dead fish were covered with a phosphorescent glow when the boat swayed towards the moon.

Then the moonlight faded and dawn came over the sea. The sun rose in the east and its rays began to dance on the black canvas. Michael was the first to awaken. He uttered a cry of fright when he looked about him and discovered where he was. The land was now at a great distance. It was little more that a dot on the far horizon. He gripped Peter by the head with both hands.

'Wake up, Peter,' he cried. 'Oh! Wake up. Something terrible has happened.'

Thinking he was at home in bed, Peter tried to push Michael away and to turn over on his other side.

'It's not time to get up yet,' he muttered.

When he finally was roused and realized what had happened, he was much more frightened than Michael.

'Oh! You devil!' he said. 'We pulled anchor. We're lost.'

There was a look of ignorant panic in his small eyes. Michael bit his lip, in an effort to keep himself from crying out loud. It was a great shock to find that Peter, who had always been the leader of the two comrades and who had never before shown any signs of fear, was now in panic.

'We're not lost,' he said angrily.

'Will you look at where the land is?' cried Peter. 'Will you look?'

Suddenly Michael felt that he no longer wanted to cry. His eyes got a hard and almost cruel expression in them.

'Stand up, will you?' he said sharply. 'Let me pull the rope.'

Peter looked at Michael stupidly and got out of the way. He sat on the forward transom, while Michael hauled in the anchor rope.

'What could we do?' he said. 'We're lost unless they come and find us. We could never row that far with the wind against us.'

'Why don't you give me a hand with the rope and stop whinging?' cried Michael angrily.

Peter was roused by this insult from a boy whom he had until now been able to dominate. He glared at Michael, spat on his hands and jumped to his feet.

'Get out of my way,' he said gruffly. 'Give me a hold of that rope. Look who's talking about whinging.'

With his superior strength, Peter quickly got the rope and anchor stone into the bow. Then the two of them hauled in the lines. They did not trouble to wind them on the frames but left them lying in a tangled heap on the bottom.

'Hurry up,' Peter kept saying. 'We have to hurry out of here.'

Still roused to anger by Michael's insult, he got out his oars and turned the bow towards the dot of land on the horizon. Michael also got out his oars.

'Left hand on top,' Peter shouted, 'and give it your strength. Stretch to it. Stretch.'

'We better take it easy,' Michael said. 'We have a long way to go.'

'Stretch to it, I tell you,' Peter shouted still more loudly. 'Give it your strength if you have any.'

As soon as he found the oars in his hands, as a means of escape from what he feared, he allowed himself again to go into a panic. He rowed wildly, leaping from the transom with each stroke.

'Why can't you keep time?' Michael shouted at him. 'Keep time with the stern. You'll only kill yourself that way.'

'Row, you devil and stop talking,' cried Peter. 'Give length to your stroke and you'll be able to row with me.'

'But you're supposed to keep with me,' Michael said. 'You're supposed to keep with the stern.'

Suddenly Peter pulled so hard that he fell right back off the transom into the bow. One of the oars jumped off the thole pin as he fell backwards. It dropped over the side of the boat and began to drift astern. Michael turned the boat and picked up the oar.

'Don't do that again,' he said as he gave the oar to Peter, 'Listen to what I tell you and row quietly.'

Peter looked in astonishment at the cruel eyes of his

comrade. He was now completely dominated by them.

'It's no use, Michael,' he said dejectedly. 'You see the land is as far away as ever. It's no use trying to row.'

'We'll make headway if we row quietly,' Michael said. 'Come on now. Keep time with the stern.'

Now that he had surrendered to the will of his comrade, Peter rowed obediently in time with the stern oars. The boat began to make good way.

'That's better,' Michael said, when they had been rowing a little while. 'They'll soon be out looking for us. All we have to do is keep rowing.'

'And where would they be looking for us?' said Peter. 'Sure nobody saw us leave the port.'

'They'll see the boat is gone,' Michael said. 'Why can't you have sense? I bet they're out looking for us now. All we have to do is to keep rowing quietly.'

'And how would they see us?' Peter said after a pause. 'We can hardly see the land from here, even though it's so big. How could they see this curragh from the land and it no bigger than a thimble on the water?'

Michael suddenly raised his voice and said angrily:
'Is it how you want us to lie down and let her drift away until we die of hunger and thirst? Stop talking and row quietly. You'll only tire yourself out with your talk.'

'Don't you be shouting at me, Michael O'Hara,' Peter

cried. You better watch out for yourself. Is it how you think I'm afraid of you?'

They rowed in silence after that for more than two hours. The boat made good way and the land became much more distinct on the horizon. It kept rising up from the ocean and assuming its normal shape. Then Peter dropped his oars and let his head hang forward on his chest. Michael went forward to him.

'I'm thirsty.' Peter said. 'I'm dying with the thirst. Is there any sign of anybody coming?'

'There is no sign yet, Peter,' Michael said gently. 'We have to have courage, though. They'll come all right. Let you lie down in the bow for a while. I'll put your jersey over your face to keep the sun from touching you. That way you won't feel the thirst so much. I heard my father say so.'

He had to help Peter into the bow, as the older boy was completely helpless with exhaustion. He pulled off Peter's jersey and put it over his face.

‘Lie there for a while.’ he said, ‘and I’ll keep her from drifting. Then you can spell me.’

He returned to his seat and continued to row. He suffered terribly from thirst. He was also beginning to feel the first pangs of sea-hunger. Yet he experienced an exaltation that made him impervious to this torture. Ever since his imagination had begun to develop, he had been plagued by the fear that he would not be able to meet danger with courage. Even though he deliberately sought out little dangers and tested himself against them without flinching, he continued to believe that the nervousness he felt on these occasions was a sign of cowardice and that he would fail when the big test came.

Now that the big test had come, he experienced the first dark rapture of manhood instead of fear. His blue eyes were no longer soft and dreamy. They had a look of sombre cruelty in them, the calm arrogance of the fighting male. His mind was at peace, because he was now free from the enemy that had lurked within him. Even the pain in his bowels and in his parched throat only served to excite the triumphant will of his awakening manhood. When his tired muscles could hardly clutch the oars within his blistered palms, he still continued to row mechanically.

In the afternoon, when the village boats finally came to the rescue, Michael was still sitting on his transom, trying to row feebly. By then he was so exhausted that he did not hear the approach of the boats until a man shouted from the nearest one of them. Hearing the shout, he fell from his seat in a faint.

When he recovered consciousness, he was in the bow of his father's boat. His father was holding a bottle of water to his lips. He looked up into his father's rugged face and smiled when he saw there was no anger in it. On the contrary, he had never before seen such tenderness in his father's stern eyes.

'Was it how you dragged anchor?' his father said.

Although his upper lip was twitching with emotion, he spoke in a casual tone, as to a comrade.

'It could happen to the best of men,' the father continued thoughtfully after Michael had nodded his head. 'There's no harm done though, thank God.'

He put some clothes under the boy's head, caressed him roughly and told him to go to sleep. Michael closed his eyes. In another boat, Peter's father was shouting in an angry tone.

Michael opened his eyes again when his father and the other men in the boat had begun to row. He looked at the muscular back of his father, who was rowing in the bow seat. A wave of ardent love for his father swept through his blood, making him feel tender and weak. Tears began to stream from his eyes, but they were tears of joy because his father had looked at him with tenderness and spoken to him as to a comrade.